This book belongs to

. . . .

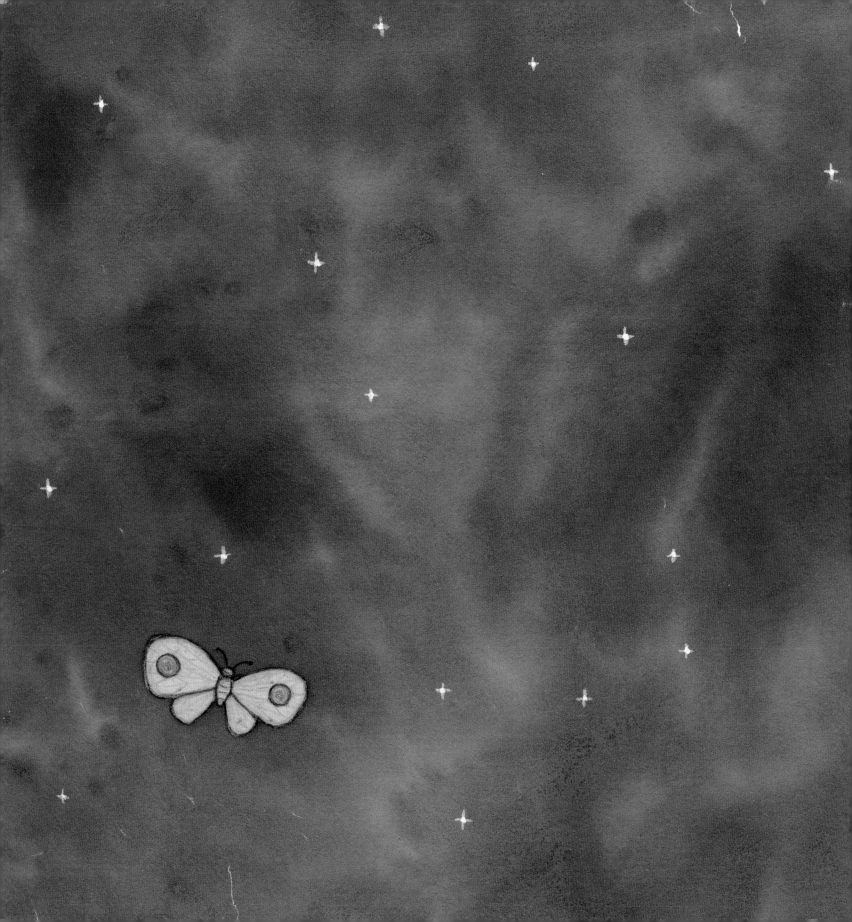

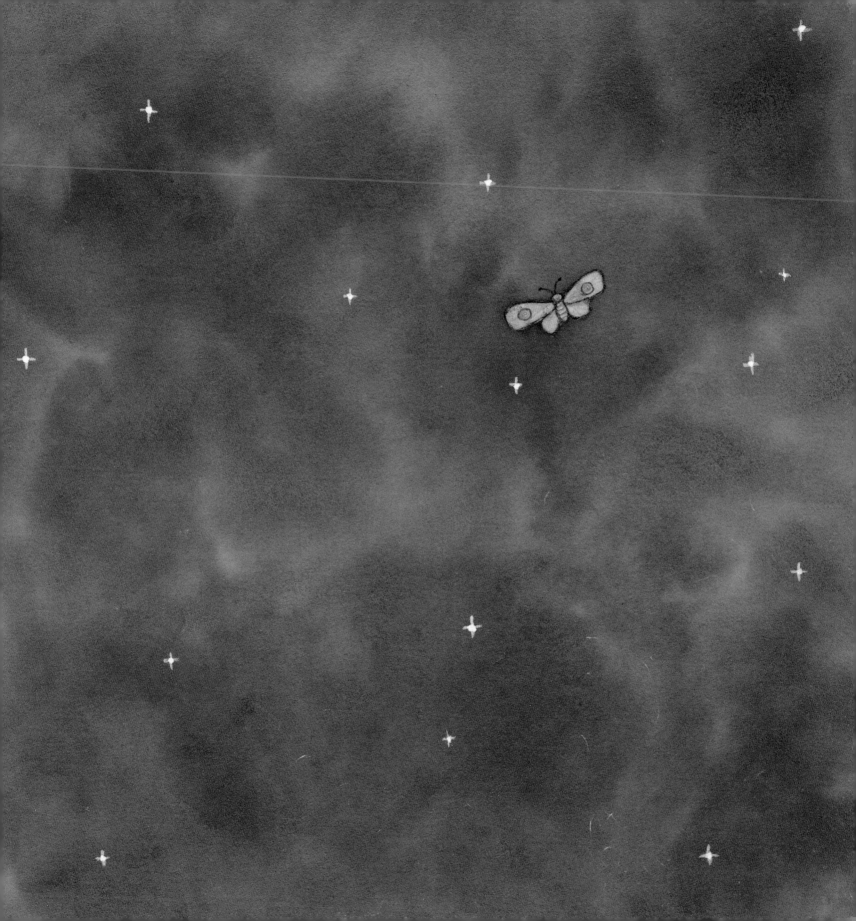

For my Mum and Dad. Always near — A.S.
For Elizabeth Nancy Georgina, my lovely Mum — L.M.

OXFORD
UNIVERSITY PRESS

Great Clarendon Street, Oxford OX2 6DP

Oxford University Press is a department of the University of Oxford.
It furthers the University's objective of excellence in research, scholarship,
and education by publishing worldwide in

Oxford New York

Auckland   Cape Town   Dar es Salaam   Hong Kong   Karachi
Kuala Lumpur   Madrid   Melbourne   Mexico City   Nairobi
New Delhi   Shanghai   Taipei   Toronto

With offices in
Argentina   Austria   Brazil   Chile   Czech Republic   France   Greece
Guatemala   Hungary   Italy   Japan   Poland   Portugal   Singapore
South Korea   Switzerland   Thailand   Turkey   Ukraine   Vietnam

Text copyright © Amber Stewart 2013
Illustrations copyright © Layn Marlow 2013
The moral rights of the author and artist have been asserted

Database right Oxford University Press (maker)

First published 2013

British Library Cataloguing in Publication Data available

ISBN: 978-0-19-275840-8 (hardback)
ISBN: 978-0-19-275841-5 (paperback)

10 9 8 7 6 5 4 3 2 1

Printed in China

Paper used in the production of this book is a natural, recyclable product made
from wood grown in sustainable forests. The manufacturing process conforms
to the environmental regulations of the country of origin

Too Small
for my
Big Bed

**AMBER
STEWART**

**LAYN
MARLOW**

OXFORD
UNIVERSITY PRESS

As Mummy kissed Piper
goodnight, she said to him,
'If you wake in the night, don't
come straight into Mummy's bed.

Try counting to more than ten.
Maybe that will help you fall
back to sleep in your own bed.'

When Piper *did* wake in the night,
he tried counting . . .

1 2 3 4 5 6 7 8 9 10 . . .

10 and a bit . . .

10 and a bit more . . .

10 and a big bit more.

But he was still awake. And a wide-awake Piper
didn't want to be alone in the deep dark night.
'I counted to more than ten,' he whispered as
he snuggled in beside his mummy.

'What a clever little cub you are,'
she sighed.

But Piper was already fast asleep
— spread out like a small star.

In the morning, Mummy took Piper to the Golden Grasslands.

Piper pounced and jumped until he needed to stop for a rest. 'Today, I jumped higher than ever!' he said happily.

'I know,' smiled Mummy. 'I've been watching. You jumped so high, and you did it all by yourself.'
'All by myself'!' laughed Piper.

But that night Piper still didn't want
to be all by himself in the deep dark.

The next day, Mummy took Piper climbing
along Red Rock Ridge.

Piper bounded easily to the top. 'Mummy!' he called,
'Look at me. I'm going to be the king of the castle!'

'I know!' smiled Mummy.
'I'm watching . . .

You've climbed so far, and
you've done it all by yourself.'

'All by myself!'
laughed Piper.

'Tonight, Piper,' said Mummy, as they padded homewards, 'if you wake in the night, try thinking about how high you jumped and how far you climbed — all by yourself. Then perhaps staying in your own bed — all by yourself — will seem easier.'

Piper didn't look sure. 'In the deep dark night,'
he whispered, 'my bed feels too big.'
'It's not as big as my bed,' said Mummy gently.
'But when I climb into your bed, Mummy,' said Piper,
'you are near, to take away the bigness.'

Mummy and Piper stopped at their favourite pond.

While they drank, Mummy asked, 'How do you know I am near now, my clever little cub?'

'I can see your face wobbling in the water,' said Piper.

'If you keep your eyes closed, and I am quieter
than the smallest cricket,' asked Mummy,
'*then* how do you know I am near?'

Piper thought, and waited, and sniffed the air.
'I can just feel you, Mummy,' he smiled.
'I can feel you are near.'

'I'll never be far away,' she said,
as they lay in the evening sun.

'Mummies never are.'

When Piper woke that night, he looked into
the deep dark and . . .

though he couldn't see his mummy,

he could feel the cool night air
spreading her love around him.

And he knew that she was near.

So Piper snuggled down further in his own bed, and started counting to more than ten.

But he only managed to count as far as 1 2 3 before he was fast asleep . . .

right through till morning.

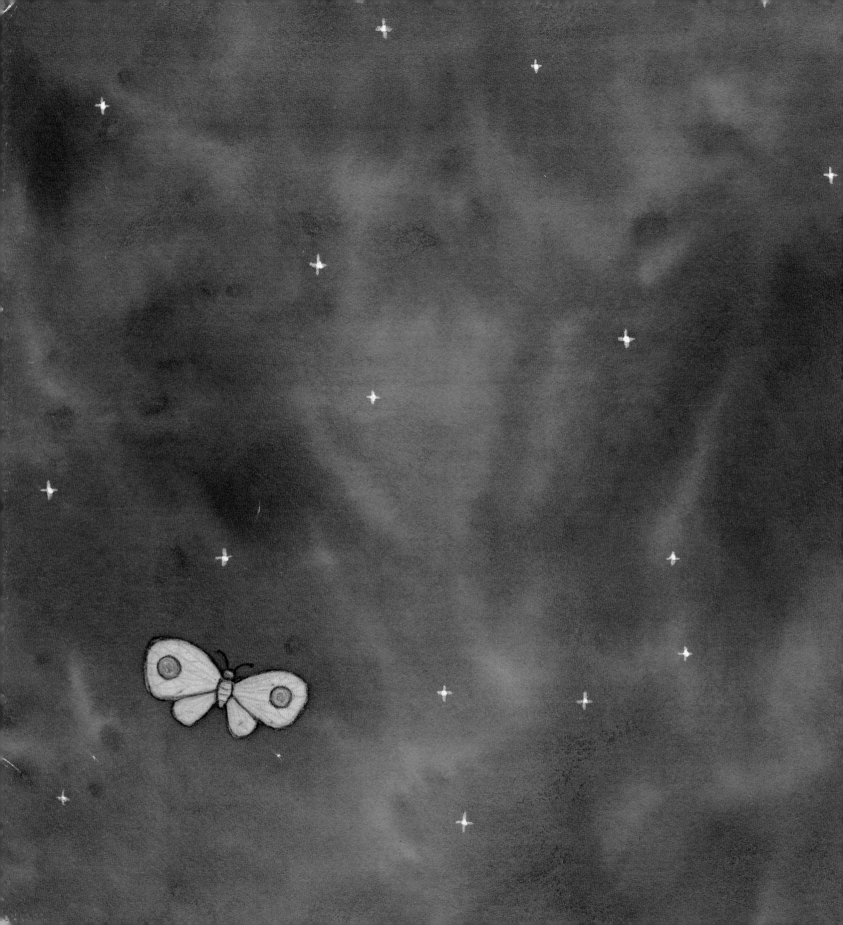

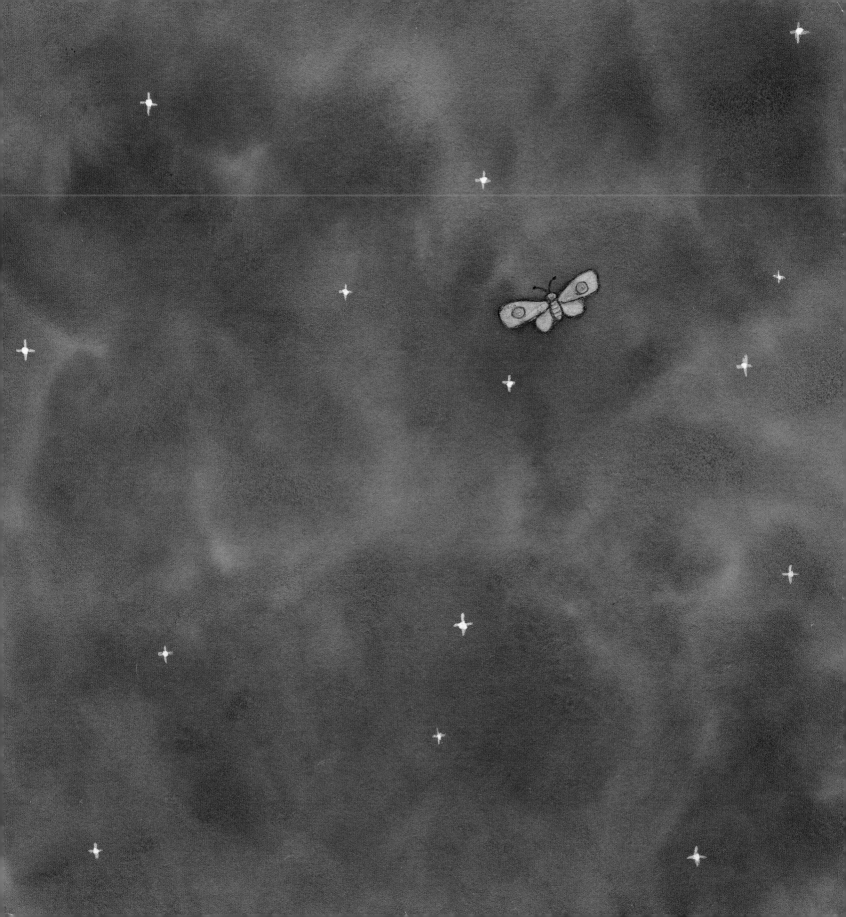